Cover: "Firelight"
 Helen Morrissey Rizzuto

*In Eamon Grennan's ennobling poem The Cave Painters,
the image of firelight is pivotal. The cover of this book pays
tribute to Mr. Grennan's poem and to the tenacity each of us
harbors in times of darkness and devastation, to go on.*

A LIGHT IN THE WINDOW
Winter Tales
Volume II

A Light in the Window – Winter Tales
Volume Two

A Light in the Window – Winter Tales is a series of chapbooks: poetry, fiction and the occasional essay. Volume One is a prize-winning short story titled *Bowie and the Beast* adapted into an illustrated book one can tuck into one's pocket. The second volume OUTPOSTS – suggesting those remote and isolated existential frontiers we all experience – consists of four flash fictions and thematically related works. Each story, poem, observation and image shines a light on the private world of an individual facing a personal outpost. Some of these tales will feel familiar, and others, global. Each, in its own way, will revisit history and through the lens of time, bring the past clearly into the present.

This is a small collection intended to awaken, comfort and inspire at this profoundly challenging moment in which so many of us find ourselves on an outpost, or several outposts, we probably never would have imagined.

Helen Morrissey Rizzuto is a poet, writer, educator and artist who has taught at Hofstra University, CUNY Queens College and for New York State Council on the Arts, as resident poet and writer. Her work explores the interrelationship of time and place, and her 'traveling exhibit' Form and Image: Graphite Works on Paper and the Worlds They Reflect consists of subjects as varied as Renaissance botanicals; the haunted underground portals of Southampton, the United Kingdom, and the famous and forgotten figures and cityscapes of her native New York City, in short, all manner of being that her pencil can bring to life from her observations, poems and stories. Some of these renderings appear within these pages. She welcomes you to OUTPOSTS.

Also by Helen Morrissey Rizzuto

"Sometimes," said the horse.
"Sometimes what?" asked the boy.
"Sometimes just getting up
        and carrying on is
            brave and magnificent."

Charles Mackesy
The Boy, the Mole, the Fox and the Horse

OUTPOSTS

By

Helen Morrissey Rizzuto

for Tommy
our North Star

INTRODUCTION

OUTPOSTS, the second volume in this series, continues to explore themes of isolation and inclusion, themes that gently engage us in exploring who we are, whom we become, and how, in the process, we co-create this planet we share and call home. In volume1 *Bowie and the Beast*, a young man living on the periphery in New York City not only is made visible, but is reached out to by someone he believes to be a 'spaceman' – in actuality, David Bowie on the evening Mr. Bowie died. The story suggests that relationships we have forged with those who have gone from here - and in this case, even relationships we have not - can be just as viable, valuable and life affirming.

Each story in OUTPOSTS is a momentary 'flash' illuminating a particular and personal 'outpost' but a spark that reminds us that we are here together, possessing and performing different roles at different moments, serving varied purposes in one another's lives, most of which we will never be aware. No need. We are all necessary; we all matter, as these stories will affirm. Each tale acknowledges that 'outpost' sense of alienation, of feeling cut off from everyone and everything we know, but each one holds something else as well, something infinitesimal perhaps, hidden for the reader to discover, and use.

Each character's story can be crystallized within a single word: *abandoned, lonely, windswept, surreal*, the way a figure in a snow-globe is encapsulated in the glass of a single fixed moment, but if the existential experience of the pandemic – that other global outpost – taught us anything, it reminded us that we are, by nature, a tribal species, and therein lies the grace of possibility or the eternal nightmare of Sartre's *No Exit*. The choice is ours to make.

The outposts you're about to visit include a sparse, crudely fashioned burrow in the sand under a dilapidated boardwalk with its penny arcade and amusements, its shouts and squeals coloring the night. An eccentric woman lives here in the dark underneath the planks, just within the sounds of the surf where she is often visited at daybreak by the terrors of her past that take the form of visions.

The second outpost is a gravel path leading to a footbridge at the far end of a desolate saltmarsh. Until an unlikely stranger enters the scene and comes upon the grotesque discovery hidden in the marsh, the only witness to a shattered dream is the osprey guarding its family in their high-pitched aerie.

The third outpost is a battered backyard shed once filled with lawn furniture and tools; its doors, now relying on a single rusty hinge, are blown open by the relentless wind. A catastrophic storm made landfall overnight and swept everything, and almost everyone, out to sea. Our guide through this dystopian universe is a young girl whose recollection of a strange song will haunt her, but provide a vestige of hope and the resolve to go on.

The fourth story is one we all share, one that ultimately brings us together and reminds us that the darkness is real, but more important, the darkness is also the cue for us to pull out our unlikeliest gifts, the ones we think we don't possess, the ones we think don't matter at all: a few written words, a sketch, a square of chocolate, a song. Fiction or not, the twentieth-century modernist writer Virginia Woolf taught us, *all of it* is *real*. OUTPOSTS is simply another word for *here*.

* Beneath the Wizard Ballroom *

Wizard Balls was so close to the Penny Arcade up on the boardwalk that people wondered how they were able to co-exist. In the daytime, you hardly noticed the place, but when night came, you could see the Wizard Ballroom for a good mile, the way it lit up that part of the boardwalk like the opening night of famous films in the old days, with those searchlights climbing high into the sky. From the outside, the Ballroom looked as tiny as Seymour's Blintzes next door, but more intriguing with its coral, fuchsia, neon green and canary balls strung from silver tracks whizzing and humming and butterfly-winging into you on your journey through the Troubled Forest to visit who else, but the Wizard.

A creature called "Charade" always ushered everyone inside. No one knew exactly why he was called Charade, or if he was even human. He was a strange looking creature, and because he never said a single word, someone started calling him Charade and the name just stuck. The Wizard was another story. According to town lore, and more likely, the owners who weren't beneath making a buck, the Wizard was a much more diminished version of the oracle of Delphi. He would make clear to you a secret you had to face – they said he'd breathe it out onto the cold sapphire night-air.

While many braved the fiber-optic filaments of chance and visited the Wizard out of curiosity, or just for fun, it was the strangers who went as believers. Everyone else was there to catch a glimpse of Xiao Mei, the mysterious woman who was rumored to live beneath Wizard Balls … even in winter, underneath that part of the boardwalk, in the sand. All sorts of stories circulated about Xiao Mei, but Xiao Mei was much more pragmatic than the townsfolk. She believed they were as good as damned.

It was said that she had a paisley mind. That's what one of those high school students had written about her for his school newspaper. "Xiao Mei, whose last name is unknown, with her psalms and her chanting and her sideshow life outside the Wizard Ballroom, is a study in contradictions." Xiao Mei liked that piece about her – the newspaper piece and the piece inside her that matched up with it – her paisley mind.

The boy didn't come around anymore, but Xiao Mei was used to things coming and going, appearing and disappearing, the whole world a sorcerer's bag of tricks just spilled out on the road, she sometimes thought, though as quickly as that thought would come, she'd look around her, from left to right, the murmuring sea behind her with its muffled waves crashing the shore. When she was sure no one had heard, she'd open up her prayer book and begin to chant. That was all she really wanted – to be left alone to chant, to recite her psalms and fill her head with angels and golden swords and pastures with gentle sheep, to crowd out the boat and everyone who washed overboard into the dark night of the sea. It wasn't easy, living so near the ocean and gaining the notoriety that a small seacoast town's school newspaper could conjure.

Sometimes, at dawn, from underneath the boardwalk, she saw them floating out there on the breakers like driftwood, or like those belly up white fish she recalled seeing as a child - leprous pale ghosts.

Still, she liked that piece about her mind, and she liked the young man who had written it. Finbar O' something was his name. *Finn*, they called him, and she liked that too, because it made him a part of her world without even knowing it - a strange, savage, saving part.

* Flight *

This short-cut through the salt marsh wasn't a good idea, she thought, as she pulled her coat tighter about her in the dark, but the desolate beauty of the marsh, with winter still clinging in small pockets of snow, told her otherwise. The tidal pools were silver, the sky-shifting reflections of greys and blues easting themselves across the water. Dense clusters of cord grass lined the path to the osprey nest, a towering ominous totem that stood black against the early morning sky. These were the images she would use to bring an ancient Chinese art to life.

In twenty minutes, her students would build their shadow puppet theatres, their puppetry and their sets: an ogre, a flying bird, a tower... and there her thoughts stopped.

On the path beyond the footbridge littered with broken shells lay something pale and twisted that even in the lingering moonlight clearly didn't belong. It wasn't the wrack that sometimes washed in, or the occasional odd section of raft or shingle of wood. The sun wasn't up yet, so she edged closer, cautiously. And then recoiled. In front of her, lay an outstretched arm, its shirt torn away from any shoulder, its hand reaching...

The movement of water molecules in human cells brings about change, and just as subtle, the movement of her mind left the sheared off arm with its wanting hand to an assumed past and an unknown future. Other scattered remains would be discovered. She knew this without knowing how; the police would have to be called, an investigation begun.

In time, they would piece together the Russian cigarettes, the prayer-beads and coins, and the lack of identification. A person halfway around the world had awakened that morning, realized time had grown short, and knew he had to leave. He would climb unseen into that chrysalis of a wheel-well, ascend in a roar of engines, freeze in the plunging temperatures and be catapulted to the ground as the landing gear finally dropped in a new world. He would not know any of this beforehand. Risk demands faith.

In the classroom, later that morning, she would banish the gruesome image on the footbridge to the outer reaches of her thoughts. She would join her students, cutting parchment for the curtain of her Chinese shadow puppet theatre. Deftly, she would create the dark figures: the ogre, the bird and the tower, and then glue these to their wooden sticks, and yet, suddenly, without any warning, as if compelled by some unseen, unacknowledged force, she picked up her scissors again and this time, cut the black leather precisely, painstakingly. When she was finished, she would study this final piece – the hand in her hand – reaching out - as if the possible were still possible.

Remembering
[The Blitz, Southampton, Winter 1940]

in the old films
those grainy black and white
and mostly European
there was always a war
and a street
left bereft

of houses, shops, homes, children
running off to schoolyards and
parents returning home from work
with lunch pails or brisket
    in butcher wrap held close to the heart
inside - empty ramekins on wooden tables,
the coal-stoves left unlit, the head of the household
the household itself
clearly gone -

    II
sitting in the cheap seats of dark cinemas
we could feel the desolation, the absence
death enforces when it enters our own households
clothes left on hangers
closets growing old around them

but in those films
there was one scene
as unexpected as the sound of
a far off bell out at sea

it might have taken place in a café
or an underground club
with Marlene and the Resistance in Berlin

more often than not, the camera
made its way down that ravaged street
of smoldering remains
of lives once lived, and panned in

on an old man strumming a balalaika or
a woman playing the broken keys of a salvaged accordion
like that imp of a fiddler high on a rooftop
wailing against the dark, defying night with song

Variation on a Theme
[for the people of the Ukraine, Gaza
and all war-torn places globally, present day]

Somewhere in this backlit world
A young woman
With an accordion or violin
Makes her way down a street

Bombs have torn doors
Off shops and houses, and children
From their parents' arms overnight

Behind her in the early light, towers
Of rubble smolder
And smoke rises
And those who survive
Come out to investigate

The young woman, undaunted, plays her music
And the scene unfolds
A portion at a time, like

One of those accordion drawings
Young students diligently design
The kind that reveal

A wing of a building, then a string of buildings
And nearby
       a river, a park, an ice-rink where
people gathered unaware that
this was Atlantis and they were
                    skating across time

only the street musician passes
        from her world
into ours and settles

in a corner of the mind
where even death can be romanticized
for a time

But she is only an image on celluloid
        and will be gone when the lights come up

All that remains, all that always remains
So remember this, and hum, sing, *play it to be heard*
Is the song

Thistle
Resilience

* After the Storm. ... *

It has all passed, in successive waves,
   just as the useless ciphers of sea foam pass...
                                    Jorge Carrera Andrade

After the storm, everything was wiped away – mother, father, the house by the sea where people had come to celebrate the holidays, and where the girl and her family had studied, played and partied. After the storm all of this was gone... all except the young girl. So many people in the village had been taken... the butcher, the watchmaker with the turn in his far-reaching eye, the ragman who wheeled his cart and sang his strange scratchy song along the back roads, the doctor with the small lit sign outside his door that blew on and off in the wind, and the nuns that floated like black ghosts across the road into the darkened church without ever touching the ground... The water broke down the doors in the evening, when the wave made shore, and dragged them off.

All of them. Swept out to sea.

The girl was alone, out in the road, stepping over the broken yellow keys of the piano her father had painted what felt like a thousand doors to be able to afford; stepping over the shattered statue of the Virgin and the soggy pages of poems in the few small volumes they could afford, poems she would take to bed with her each night for news of other lives, other worlds, that she could climb into and out of, at will. Now, she was alone with only her thoughts. She must find shelter. The winter winds and snows were coming. She could feel them even now.

At first, Time moved like a lumbering giant who would drop down wherever he pleased, to nap. As the girl moved on into this new present, she could smell winter out on the dark roads, especially early in the morning and late at night. She could feel those winds and the snow squalls they would bring, as she walked the now unfamiliar streets, passing the one small café that had stood its ground, a place where neighbors came seeking more comfort than information. At night, the cold was more insistent. The girl could feel winter waiting, just outside the gates, where a few remaining neighbors lit fires in the makeshift stoves the sea had tossed back onto land.

That first day, the girl had found what had been a neighbor's shed – it was grown over with vines and straggly blood-colored dead leaves, but other than the darkness, and a door with a loose hinge that she was able to tighten by using her fingers and a few strong twigs, the place would be fine. It was out of the elements, and the wild animals' foraging, and she found ways to keep herself warm.

People from neighboring villages had come to town with blankets and jugs of water and vegetables and fruits from their gardens, so the girl had joined her remaining neighbors and walked the miles into what once had been their town. She dragged along a twisted shopping cart, and filled it with the clothing and blankets and foods that wouldn't perish that people had brought. The boxes of matches, she tucked into her deep pockets.

That night, in the small shed in the dark, except for the dim light of the candle that sent shadows climbing up the walls, the girl decided that she would not yet say goodbye. Her parents might not have died; they might have survived that monstrous wave and been carried to another part of the world.

Her mother had survived it once before, when she was a young girl herself. She had seen the destruction of everyone and everything she had ever known; she had suckled on the tits of tornadoes, met dolphins scrambling up out of the sea, and even though sometimes only the marsh-birds of the flyway could decipher the unwieldy current of her thoughts whenever she would speak to her neighbors of the storm, she never stopped trying to warn them. At night, she would often sing the girl a song – a strange mournful song in a foreign idiom the girl could not understand. Over time, the girl would come to think of it as a prayer, something her mother seemed to be weaving together with her voice, speaking to whoever was out there, to keep her daughter safe and warm... a Storm-Woman's song.

In the beginning, people continued to come with water and food, and after many months of candles and cold, they brought electricity – lights and heat to light the communal stove. The village was coming back, never to what it had been, it would never come back to that, but everything – every small move forward that gave them hope – was *something*.

So this is how it would be, she told herself - picking up the broken crockery of their lives, putting what they could back together, and hoping and praying the glue would hold. And for some time, it did.

It is now closing in on ten years since that wave came and tore the village from its moorings. Villagers began to rebuild and others came for a time and helped, and then the wave hit somewhere else, and again, somewhere else, and work slowed down as those who'd helped moved on to help others. Years passed and people came once more, this time with big machines and promises.

In the end, although it appeared to be thriving, nothing had truly changed, not for the better. The village was even more vulnerable. The wise ones who knew how to build a seawall were never listened to, and knowing what they did, they moved away; the village elders sold off land they didn't own, and large cranes moved in. You can see them now, down where they put up two gigantic structures – like ancient rusting dinosaurs drifting nearer the sea.

Those who have been here from the beginning look to the sea. The winter winds and snows are coming. You can smell them on the air. They will be here soon. Down where the robbers patrol the sand, the machinery is so loud. No one can hear the Storm Woman's song.

A poem is a window through which everything
that passes can be seen anew
Lawrence Ferlinghetti

and sometimes, like a poem, a pandemic...

Sometimes he wondered how all of them were – if they were. It was strange to be carrying them still, even now – the Italian nurse who worked so many shifts that she didn't see her children for days, and even worse, nights. The sky over Rome would barely be dawning when she would get herself out of bed and back out on the road, but not before gently blowing each of them a kiss. How she longed to touch them, breathe in the sweet air of their presence; instead, she would place another kiss – a chocolate one - beside each of their plates where they would find them, and only then would she make her way down to the silent street and her car.

And then there was the man he had encountered on a side street back home here in the city, a man screaming, *Oh my God, oh God, this is real*! His screams shattered the morning stillness, but didn't interrupt the silent queue of ghosts wheeling gurney after gurney - death-carts - carrying what looked like sacks of laundry.

Listen to me, everyone. This is real, he shouted. *This is happening. Here. Right now.* And then he took out his phone and videoed the gruesome procession and the first of the portable morgues - the refrigerator trucks lined up along the street, waiting; the forklifts were already at work.

Yes, there was the nurse and then this dark ancient seer and there were others - some, like the children, he wouldn't allow himself to think about - but he carried them all, remembering each of them, and among them, the priest who had told him that on those early evenings, standing on that rooftop, on all the rooftops with all the other stranded souls in the city cheering and banging on their pots some fanatical semblance of Morse code, he had been driven very close to despair. Yes, the priest was a part of him, too.

But Time had passed, and was passing, or he was finally passing through Time, the dark cavern of it. It reminded him now of that tunnel in Central Park that echoes with each footfall, thread of laughter, bouncing ball, and barking dog, Everyone - the entire parade - tap-dancing, passing into the future.

Yes, tonight he carried them all inside him. While everyone else seemed to have moved on, it was taking him much longer.

He made his way up the street, pulled out the fob that unlocked the heavy front door of the pre-war Art-Deco building he called home. Upstairs, inside his apartment, under the warmth of his reading lamp, he sat surrounded by his books – his faithful companions - and he decided to visit the one person he would not allow to die, even if this stranger had already left the earth, which he doubted.

The old man was someone he had seen once on a midtown street shaded by scaffolding, an old man pushing a tall upright piano through the mid-day crowds, an image that would come back to him at odd times, like now. Unwieldy, worn, wiry and strong, the upright was much like the old man. Tonight, that homeless troubadour who had wheeled that piano through the busiest streets in the busiest of cities, going corner to corner to who knows where, was inviting him to join him.

He could feel himself smiling for the first time in a very long time, traveling without need of transport. This was something new, a gift. This would be the first time he would hear that battered beautiful upright sing. Yes, it was time for song.

for all the guardian spirits out there, the living, and those
who have moved on

AFTERWORD

Outposts, those remote and often inaccessible places that exist all around us take innumerable forms: the craggy aerie of medieval monks illuminating and preserving civilization; the sacred sites and mountain shrines; the forest rangers' lookout tower, the lighthouse with its saving signal, the space station which looks to the future. Beyond these are the outposts of the heart that Chekhov and others have written about in such tender and luminous prose and poetry. The outposts of fear, loneliness, displacement and personal loss that we all experience are often far less visible, but undeniably as universal.

Some years ago, when I was researching the rich and raveled history of the port city of Southampton in the United Kingdom, I reached the 14th century just as the pandemic of 2020 erupted here. Southampton, in the 14th century, is believed to have been the entry point for the ongoing bubonic plague that ravaged England and well beyond.

The similarities between that period and this remain daunting. In spite of our countless life saving modern advances, the death pits and associated horrors of that earlier period, captured in artistic renderings, bore a viscerally shocking resemblance to the onslaught of all that we would witness and experience, seven centuries later. Likewise, each story in this small volume is a counterpart to that of the larger reality.

Pandemics come in many guises, and catastrophes – personal, communal and global – like those we experience today, wake us up to the realization that the life and lives we've been given, and all those lives we hold close and often take for granted, are precious and fragile.

Catastrophic storms will continue to exist, and oppression so great that the desperation to flee – or stay - will far outweigh the dangers. Likewise, PTSD and the heartache that follow, but there also will exist that 'something else' alluded to earlier that we might wish to look at, because it also directly impacts our lives – and ultimately, can save them.

Like the characters in each of these works, there will be those in this world who are destined, or more likely will *choose*, to become the witnesses, guardians and repository of all that transpires: the caregivers, the listeners, the teachers and guides, the poets and makers of music, the close readers and the builders and 'rebuilders' who appear in countless unrecognized and unacknowledged forms, *every day,* even to themselves, *ourselves.* Outposts are both a necessary and inescapable part of life, but they also provide us these unparalleled opportunities for creating blueprints for the life, and lives, we want to live.

I thank you for sharing this time with me and most of all, for sharing your song.

ACKNOWLEDGMENTS

In writing a book, one willingly takes up life on an outpost. Some days the outpost may be a welcome sanctuary away from the noise of the world, but other days, it may be something very different, something far more challenging. With this in mind, I owe deep gratitude to my family, my close friends, and to all those in my life who not only understand, but often mitigate the sense of isolation the outpost experience can impose or evoke.

A special word of appreciation to

Annie, Miriam, Kathy and Linda
Hilari, Niki, Joan & Ellen
Michael and Susan Hoffman
Matthew Pravetz, O.F.M.
Robert E. Kennedy, S.J. and Morning Star Sangha
Michael Sehler, S.J.
Margaret Krug
Rosa Goeller
Olympia and George Stassinopoulos
Javier Licona
Agata Tilli
Twyla Tharp
Kat Wildish
Marie Forleo
R. J. Mackool
Nicole Vu

and to Grace Maher who with utmost patience and care
steadily guides each book into port

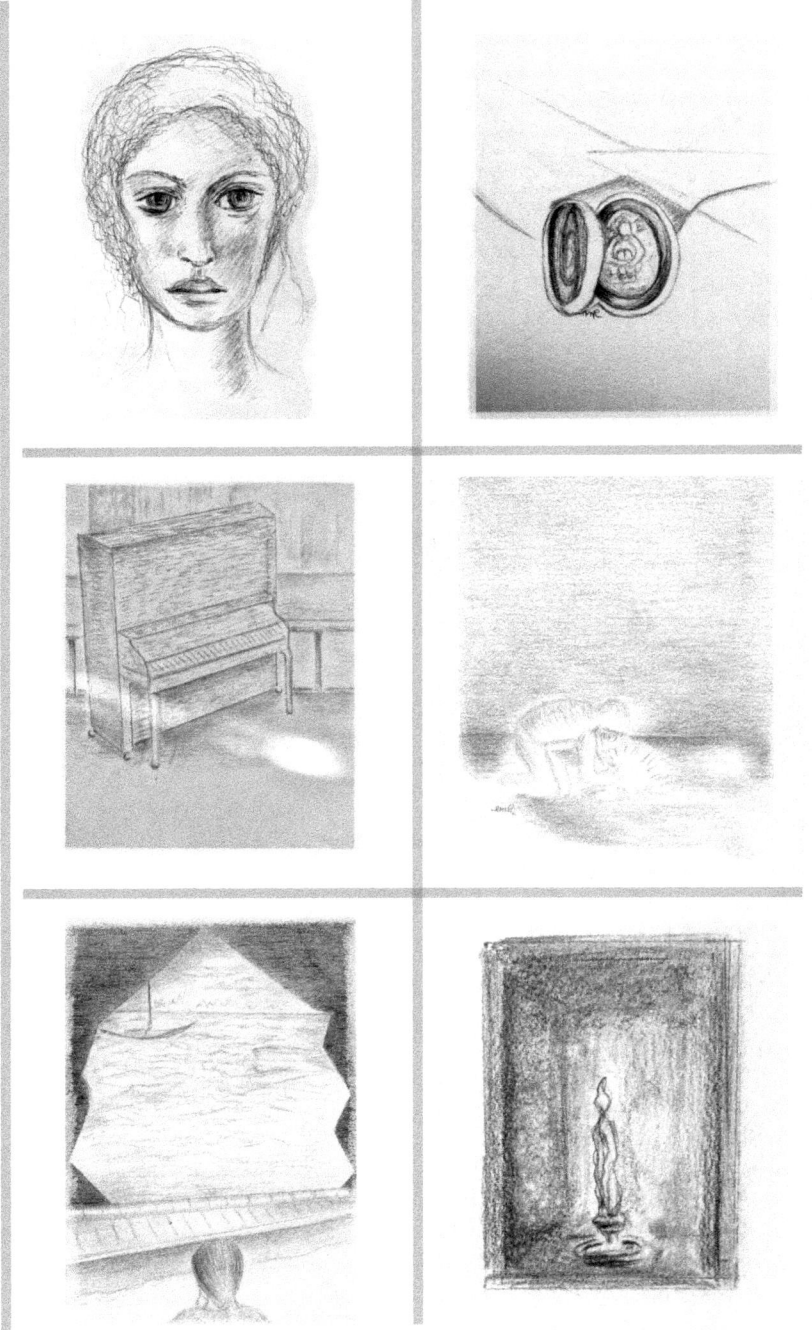